First!

Written by Kes Gray

Illustrated by Korky Paul

 Collins

It was Flynn's first day at school and he was feeling a bit nervous.

"I'm a bit nervous," he said to his mum and dad.
"What if I get something wrong?"

Flynn's mum and dad smiled. "Don't worry,
Flynn," they said. "Lots of people get things wrong
on their first day."

Police officer Julie Nicks gave a robber
an ice cream on her first day.

Rod Hod, the builder, built a house
upside down on his first day.

Ned Mutton, the farm worker, tried to milk the chickens on his first day.

Rose Trellis, the gardener, cut the flowers
instead of the grass on her first day.

Shirley Curly, the hairdresser, used
the wrong scissors on her first day.

Ravi Pastree, the cook, put jam in
the sausage rolls on his first day.

Anna Conda, the zookeeper, tried to sweep out the shark tank on her first day.

Zondor the stunt man's first day would have been his last day, if the custard had been a bit deeper.

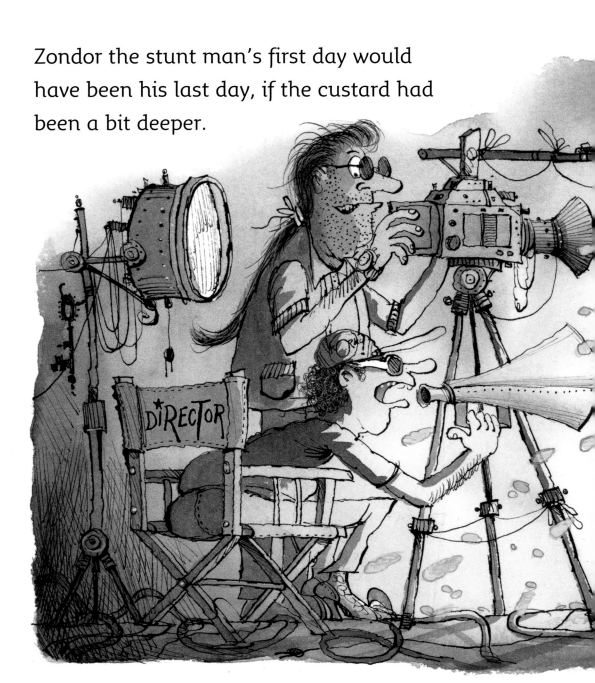

"Well, I won't do anything as silly as that on *my* first day!" smiled Flynn.

"Of course you won't ..."
said Mum and Dad ...

"... but you might want to change out of your pyjamas before you go to school!"

First day

Julie Nicks

Rod Hod

Ned Mutton

Rose Trellis

Shirley Curly

Ravi Pastree

Anna Conda

Zondor

Ideas for reading

Written by Clare Dowdall BA(Ed), MA(Ed)
Lecturer and Primary Literacy Consultant

Learning objectives: tell stories and describe incidents from own experience in an audible voice; read more challenging texts which can be decoded using acquired phonic knowledge and skills, along with automatic recognition of high frequency words; use syntax and context when reading for meaning; visualise and comment on events, characters and ideas, making links to own experiences

Curriculum links: Citizenship: Choices; People who help us

Interest words: first, nervous, wrong, police officer, builder, farm worker, gardener, hairdresser, cook, zookeeper, stunt man, custard, pyjamas

Resources: drawing materials

Word count: 209

Getting started

- Ask the children to recount their first day at school and how they felt.
- Look at the front cover together and read the title. Look at the word *First*. Practise stretching it to hear the phonemes *f-ir-s-t*.
- Read the back cover blurb together. Model using phonic skills to read new words, e.g. *nervous*.
- Discuss the information given in the blurb and ask the children to predict what they think might happen to Flynn on his first day.

Reading and responding

- Read to p7 with the children, to introduce the pattern of the text.
- Ask the children to describe what is happening in the pictures on pp6–7 and to explain what the police officer did wrong on her first day.
- In pairs, invite the children to continue reading the story aloud. Support them by helping with tricky words, encouraging them to re-read fluently.